If I Were a
KANGAROO

A Bedtime Tale

By **Mylisa Larsen**   Illustrated by **Anna Raff**

VIKING

VIKING
An imprint of Penguin Random House LLC
375 Hudson Street
New York, New York 10014

First published in the United States of America by Viking,
an imprint of Penguin Random House LLC, 2017

LIBRARY OF CONGRESS CATALOGING-IN-PUBLICATION DATA IS AVAILABLE
ISBN: 9780451469588

Special Markets ISBN: 9780451480392 Not for Resale

Manufactured in China

1 2 3 4 5 6 7 8 9 10

The artwork for this book was created with ink washes, and pen
or pencil drawings that were assembled and colored digitally.

This Imagination Library edition is published by Penguin Young Readers, a division
of Penguin Random House, exclusively for Dolly Parton's Imagination Library,
a not-for-profit program designed to inspire a love of reading and learning, sponsored
in part by The Dollywood Foundation. Penguin's trade editions of this work are
available wherever books are sold.

If I were a kangaroo,
I'd pick you up and carry you
In my pocket, sleepyhead,
And hop you gently off to bed.

If I were a giant whale,
I'd sing you songs—slow epic tales.

Fin to fin, down in the deep,
We'd drift together into sleep.

If you were a chick, my dear,
I'd cluck a cozy "We're all here,"
Close my wing-roof overhead
To make a rustling feather bed.

Squirrels cuddle in a heap,
Swaying in their nest, asleep.
If we slept in that nest up high,
The wind would sing our lullaby.

If you were a small giraffe,
My little spotted knob-kneed calf,
We'd nap together standing tall,
Rarely lying down at all.

Feet above, head down below,
Bats sleep upside down, you know.
If we were bats, at end of day,
We'd just be waking up to play.

If you were a little otter,
Side by side we'd ride the water
On a sea that never ends,
In a raft made up of friends.

If I were a mommy spider,
You would be a spider rider
Resting with your sisters, brothers,
Legs, legs, legs, next to each other.

Mom gorillas build a nest
Where babies snuggle up to rest.
If we were them, we'd curl up tight
And dream gorilla dreams all night.

But you're not fish nor bug nor bird,
So hush now, not another word.

I'll count your fingers and your toes
And kiss you gently on your nose,

Then tuck you in and hug you tight.
And whisper,
"I love you . . .
Good night."

Sleepy Animal Notes

Every night a mama **gorilla** builds a brand-new nest for herself and her baby to share. The nest might be in a tree or on the ground. The gorilla bends branches of trees or bushes and weaves them into a nest shaped like a big bowl. This gives a whole new meaning to "make your bed"!

Though **spiders** don't sleep in quite the same way as humans, they do have alternating periods of rest and activity. And spiders that live in cold climates can go into a winter sleep like hibernation. Mommy wolf spiders carry their egg sacs with them until the baby spiders hatch. Then the babies ride around on their mom's back in a big, spidery pile.

Bats sleep during the day, which is different from how most people sleep. And they sleep hanging upside down, which is *definitely* different from people. A baby bat sleeps in a nursery colony with other bat moms and babies. The baby may hang from his mom's furry tummy. While the moms are off hunting for food, the babies wait at home. When mom flies home, she can find her own little baby bat by his voice and smell, even though there are hundreds of other babies all hanging out together in a small space.

Sea otters sleep floating on their backs in the water. They often join with other otters in groups called rafts and rest together. Sometimes otters hold paws with each other to keep from floating apart while they sleep. Mom otters might wrap a strand of kelp around a baby otter's middle so the baby doesn't float away while the mom dives under the water searching for food. Baby otters often ride on their moms' tummies, floating and resting.

Squirrels carry a built-in blanket—their tails. They wrap their tails around their bodies when they sleep, like tucking themselves in. Their tails can even be an umbrella when it rains. Moms and babies sleep in nests called dreys. Built in a fork of a tree or a hollow place, dreys are made of sticks and twigs. Soft things like bird feathers and fur make the inside comfy.

Well, **giraffes** don't sleep much. Grown-up giraffes sleep less than two hours a day, mostly in five-minute naps. A giraffe can sleep standing up, with its long neck twisted to rest along its back. For the first few days after it is born, a baby giraffe stays near its mom, resting and sleeping. It may lie down to sleep more often than grown giraffes do.

Baby **chicks** have a cozy tent always waiting for them. Their moms have wide wings to snuggle under. At night (or in the rain or cold), chicks climb back into the nest, where their mom spreads her wings over all her babies, keeping them warm and dry.

For the first few weeks of a baby **whale's** life, she doesn't have enough blubber to float if she stops moving. So she naps while she swims. She'll swim a little behind her mom in the slipstream where her mom's big strokes help pull a little whale along. Since the baby is still too little to swim the long distances of their migration, she and her mom hang out for four to six weeks, swimming slowly and resting while the baby grows. There might be a whole nursery of moms and babies taking it slow together.

When a baby **kangaroo** is born, he's only as big as a lima bean, and he looks a little like a pink grub. He's bald. He can't see. Only his front legs are developed. But he uses those little front legs to climb up his mom's belly and into her pouch. There he stays, drinking milk, growing, and sleeping until finally he's big enough to stick his head out and look around. After he grows some more, he climbs out of his mom's pouch and hops around on his own. But he often climbs back into the pouch and spends a lot of time there until he's almost a year old.